Giselle the Christmas Ballet Fairy

To ballerinas everywhere

Special thanks to Rachel Elliot

ISBN 978-0-545-85203-6

10 9 8 7 6 5 4 3 2 1 16 17 18 19 20

Printed in the U.S.A. 40
First printing October 2016

Giselle the Christmas Ballet Fairy

by Daisy Meadows

Scholastic Inc.

The Fairyland Palace
Seeing Pool
Fairyland
Tippington Town

Jack Frost's Ice Castle
Well
Forget-me-not Glade
Castle Springs Ballet School
Rachel's House
Castle Springs Garden

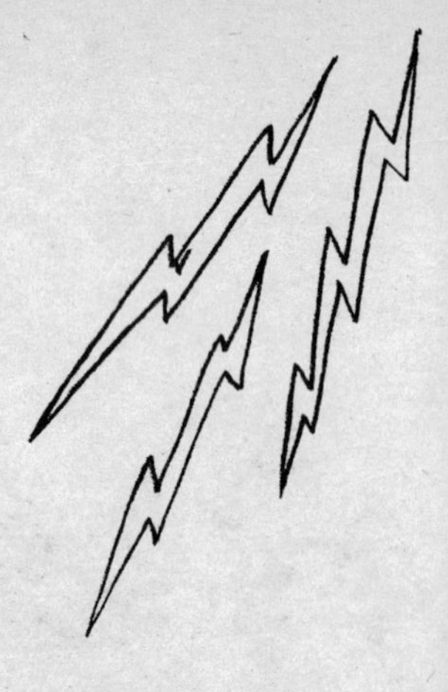

This ballet fairy know-it-all
Is in for a surprise.
When she sees Frostyev on stage,
She won't believe her eyes.

I'm the greatest! I'm the best!
But just to be quite certain,
I'll make all Christmas ballets fail
Before the final curtain!

Find the hidden letters in the stars throughout this book. Unscramble all 9 letters to spell a special ballet word!

The Magic Bottle

Contents

"It's Christmas Eve," said Rachel Walker, gazing out of her bedroom window at the snowy sky. "Santa Claus and his elves are packing the sleigh full of toys, the reindeer are getting ready for their journey . . ."

". . . And we are going to have the most amazing day ever," finished her best friend, Kirsty Tate.

Rachel turned and smiled at her. The one thing that made Christmas truly perfect was being able to share it with each other. This year was especially exciting because the girls had received a wonderful early Christmas present. Months ago, they had entered a competition called Best Friends Forever. They had had to draw a picture of each other and write one hundred words about what made their best friend special. They had forgotten all about the competition until a typed white envelope arrived, addressed to them both:

Dear Rachel and Kirsty,

Congratulations! We are delighted to tell you that you have won first prize in our Best Friends Forever competition.

Your description of your magical friendship is inspiring, and we all feel that you deserve a special day out together.

You told us that you both love dancing, so we have arranged for you to spend a day at the famous Castle Springs Ballet School.

We have also included two tickets for the evening performance of *Swan Lake*.

Have a wonderful Christmas and enjoy spending time together.

Best wishes,

Amanda Blake

Amanda Blake
Competition Manager

Rachel and Kirsty had gotten up early so that they would have plenty of time to pack their bags and decide what to wear. They were taking their ballet outfits, just in case they got the chance to dance. When they had finished breakfast, Mr. Walker drove them to the dancing school.

The Castle Springs Ballet School was very famous, and the building was extremely old and elegant. Kirsty and Rachel gazed up at its grand entrance in awe.

"Have a great day," said Mr. Walker. "I'll drop your mom off later, in plenty of time for the ballet."

The girls ran up the stone steps hand-in-hand. The door was open, and a huge hallway with black-and-white

tiles stretched out in front of them. An enormous chandelier hung from the high ceiling, twinkling brightly, and a wide staircase curved up to the next floor.

"Oh my goodness," said Kirsty. "I've got butterflies in my stomach."

"Me, too, a little bit," said Rachel with a nervous smile. "It's even more magnificent than I imagined."

Just then, a tall, willowy lady hurried toward them. She held out her arms and gave the girls a warm hug. Her silver hair was tied back in a loose ponytail, and her blue eyes sparkled.

"You must be Rachel and Kirsty," she said. "We've been looking forward to your visit very much. Congratulations on winning the prize. Friendship means a great deal to us here at Castle Springs. I am the director of the school, and my name is Sophia."

"We're really excited," said Kirsty.

"And a bit nervous!" added Rachel.

"Perhaps our prima ballerina can help calm your nerves," said Sophia, waving her arm toward the stairs.

A graceful, beautiful young woman was coming down the stairs, wearing a leotard and warm-up shorts. Her dark-brown hair was swept back under a headband, and she smiled when she saw the girls.

"Hello, my name is Penny," she said.

Rachel and Kirsty felt very excited. They knew that the prima ballerina was the best and most important dancer in the company.

"It's great to meet you," said Kirsty. "We can't wait to see you dance."

"Well, I'm looking forward to seeing *you* both dance," said Penny. "I've arranged for you to attend the *corps de ballet* rehearsal class."

The girls were thrilled. The *corps de ballet* was the group of backing dancers in the ballet company. Lots of famous ballerinas had started their dancing careers in the *corps de ballet*!

A Dancing Dream

A short time later, Rachel and Kirsty were standing in a practice room with the members of the *corps de ballet*, who were chatting quietly. Penny was sitting on a wooden chair at the side of the room. The ballet teacher clapped her hands together and everyone fell silent.

"Good morning, everyone," she said, "and a special welcome to our guests, Rachel and Kirsty. I would like to start with a little introduction to the—"

She broke off to cough into her handkerchief.

"I'm sorry," she said with a croak in her voice. "As I was saying, I would like to give the girls a little introduction to the *corps de ballet*. Most great ballerinas started out in the *corps*. The dancers here are intelligent, hard-working, patient, and disciplined. They share a group focus and they know how to work as a team."

She broke off to cough again, and Penny stood up.

"The *corps* is the heart of the company," she said. "If just one person

forgets which arm to lift or which leg to stand on, it will spoil the whole scene. Together, these dancers can make or break a performance."

The ballet teacher smiled at her.

"So, without further ado, let's start our warm-up," she said. "First position, please. And, *demi-plié*."

Rachel and Kirsty followed the instructions as well as they could.

There were a few steps and positions that they didn't know, but they were surprised by how many they recognized. The hardest part was keeping up—the professional dancers were very fast.

"I feel as if my dancing is getting better just from *watching* them," Rachel whispered to her best friend.

"Me, too," Kirsty replied. "Every single one of them is amazing!"

One of the dancers overheard and smiled at them.

"Just wait until you see Penny dance," she said. "It's like magic."

The girls smiled at each other. After all, they knew more about magic than most people! They had made friends with many fairies, and they loved sharing the secret of their exciting adventures.

After the warm-up, the class really began. Rachel and Kirsty tried to keep up, but the speed and variety of the moves was incredible. They couldn't manage all the jumps, and they hadn't expected the amount of acting the *corps* had to do. But it was very exciting to feel that, for a short while, they were swans, dancing under a magical spell.

At last, the ballet teacher called a break.

"Take five minutes and have some water," she said in a rasping voice.

Rachel and Kirsty were very glad to have a chance to rest. They went back to the changing room to grab their

water bottles, chatting about all the things they had been doing.

"You must have to be able to learn really fast to be in the *corps*," said Kirsty. "There's so much to remember!"

"I'll be watching *all* the dancers at the performance tonight, just as much as the main ballerina," said Rachel, pushing open the changing room door.

"Do you hear violins?" asked Kirsty suddenly.

Rachel listened and heard the faint sound of music.

"Do you think the class has started again already?" she asked.

Kirsty shook her head. "It sounds almost as if it's coming from your bag," she said.

"That's not possible," said Rachel, unzipping her bag to get her water. "Oh!"

As soon as her bag was open, the girls heard a loud burst of vibrant string music, and then an exquisite fairy came pirouetting out toward them. Another fairy adventure was about to begin!

A Fairy and a Frosty Problem

For a moment, Rachel and Kirsty just stared at the little fairy with their mouths open. Even for a fairy, she was so sparkly and beautiful that she almost took their breath away. She was wearing a glimmering pink leotard with a tutu, and her satin ballet shoes were pink, too. Her chestnut-brown hair gleamed, and her eyes were as bright as stars.

"Hello, Rachel and Kirsty," said the fairy. "I'm Giselle the Christmas Ballet Fairy."

"Hello, Giselle," said Kirsty. "It's wonderful to meet you—especially here!"

Giselle looked around and laughed.

"Yes," she said, "this is the kind of place I belong, whether in the human world or in Fairyland."

"You look like a prima ballerina," said Rachel.

"I look *after* prima ballerinas," Giselle said with a smile. "I take care of all dancers who perform in Christmas ballets. It is the most special time of the year for ballet, because a good performance can take everyone who sees it on a magical journey."

"You must be very busy today, on Christmas Eve," said Kirsty.

"I should be watching over all the Christmas ballets and keeping the dancers safe and healthy," said Giselle.

"But Jack Frost has made up his mind to cause trouble for me this Christmas, and he's started by stealing my magic water bottle."

"Why does he want to cause trouble for you?" Rachel asked.

Giselle did an arabesque in midair.

"Ballet positions help me to think," she said, smiling. "I think Jack Frost is angry because I tried to give him some advice. He was dancing as Frostyev in his Goblinovski Festival

Ballet, and there were a few simple ways that he could have improved his style. I was trying to help, but he took it very badly. He said I was rude and interfering, and that he was going to get back at me."

"So he took your magic bottle," said Kirsty. "What does it do?"

"It makes sure that all ballerinas feel healthy before a performance," said Giselle. "Without it, winter coughs and colds could attack the dancers and ruin the Christmas ballets. I have no idea where Jack Frost has hidden it. Even Queen Titania's Seeing Pool hasn't been able to tell us anything. So she suggested that I come to ask for your help."

"Of course we'll help you," said Rachel.

At that moment they heard the ballet teacher calling everyone back in her croaky voice. The class was about to continue.

"You finish your class," said Giselle. "I'll hide while you dance, and then maybe we could search for the magic bottle after?"

She slipped under Kirsty's ponytail and the girls ran to join the class. Most of the dancers were standing on one side of the room. Four ballerinas were in the center, their arms crossed in front of one another, holding each others' hands.

“Ah, Rachel and Kirsty,” said the ballet teacher. “We’re going to rehearse a famous scene called *danse des petits cygnes*, which means the dance of the little swans.”

The music began, and four ballerinas began to dance sideways in a line, their legs and heads moving in unison.

“They will do sixteen *pas de chat*,” the ballet teacher explained to the girls. “They must move at exactly the same time. The dance is meant to look like baby swans huddling together for protection.”

“They make it look so easy,” said Kirsty.

“That’s their skill,” said the ballet teacher, stifling a cough. “It is a tiring and challenging dance, but these girls have practiced for months, and now they are perfect. Oh!”

The ballerina at one end of the line had stumbled and fallen! The other ballerinas gathered around to make sure the fallen girl was okay. Rachel and Kirsty gasped. They hoped she hadn't injured herself!

Goblins in the Snow

The ballet teacher rapped her stick on the floor.

"Olivia, what's the matter?" she croaked.

Olivia blushed bright red.

"It's my feet, Madame," she said. "Suddenly it feels like they're covered in blisters. It's too painful to dance."

“Go and treat them at once,” said the ballet teacher. “The opening performance is just a few hours away, and we have to be ready.”

Olivia limped away, and the rehearsal continued with just three ballerinas. But the music had barely begun when the middle dancer clutched her stomach and groaned.

“Ooh, I have an awful stomachache!” she cried.

“Go and lie down, Samira,” said the ballet teacher. “Where are the understudies?”

Two other dancers stepped forward. As the ballet teacher was talking to them, the dancer next to Kirsty suddenly staggered sideways.

"Are you all right?" asked Kirsty, holding her up.

"Dizzy," murmured the dancer. "Need air."

Rachel and Kirsty helped the fainting ballerina to the school's covered patio and lowered her onto a soft chair. Then they flung open the doors to the yard and let the cold, fresh winter air flow in. The snow had stopped falling, and a few shafts of sunlight were breaking through the clouds.

"It's a pretty yard," said Rachel, looking out at the snow-covered hedges. "I bet it's full of roses in the summer."

Suddenly a distant sparkle caught their eye. At the far end of the yard was a

pond, and two figures were bending over it, wrapped in fluffy white coats. Under Kirsty's ponytail, Giselle gave a little squeak of excitement.

"Goblins!" she whispered. "Those are goblins, girls!"

The goblins were scooping up water from the pond and splashing each other.

Rachel looked down at her thin leotard and ballet shoes.

"We can't go outside dressed like this," she said. "But we *have* to find out what those goblins are doing here."

Kirsty glanced at the dizzy ballerina. She was bending forward with her eyes closed. Giselle slipped out of her hiding place and flicked her wand. A shower of silver sparkles landed on the girls, and instantly they found themselves wearing warm, fleecy jackets and wool-lined boots.

"Thank you!" whispered Kirsty.

They ran out of the school and along the snowy path that led to the pond. Giselle fluttered between them. Now that they were closer, they could see that the goblins were using drinking bottles to scoop up the water and squirt each other.

"Oh girls, those goblins have my magic bottle!" Giselle exclaimed.

Rachel marched up to one of the goblins and tapped him on the shoulder. He turned and leapt into the air in shock.

"Go away!" the goblins squawked. "Why are you poking your nose in here? Leave us alone!"

"Just give back the bottle that doesn't belong to you," said Rachel, holding out her hand.

"Oh, you mean *this* one?" asked the taller goblin in a mocking voice.

He held up his bottle and threw it to the other goblin, who caught it and waved both bottles over his head.

"Or did you mean *my* bottle?" he asked with a snicker.

"Come on, humans, keep up!"

Kirsty suddenly had an idea. She beckoned to Rachel and lowered her voice to a whisper.

"Giselle, can you use your magic to make more bottles?" she asked. "Maybe we could confuse them."

Giselle performed a graceful *pas de chat* and, with a flick of her wand, a hundred identical bottles appeared on the path in front of them.

"Want to play?" said Rachel to the goblins.

She threw a couple of the bottles to the goblins, while Kirsty picked up three of them and started to juggle. The goblins tried to catch the new bottles and dropped them all.

"Try again!" called Rachel.

She threw more bottles to the goblins... and more...and more. Then she started juggling, too. Giselle used her magic to line the path with bottles. Soon there were so many bottles on the ground and in the air that they all lost track of which one was the magic bottle!

Bottle Battle

"Stop!" the goblins screeched. "Where's our bottle?"

"It's *my* bottle," said Giselle, folding her arms and fluttering in front of them.

"But where *is* it?" asked Rachel.

With all the identical bottles on the ground, it was impossible to tell which was the magic one. The goblins

rushed around, trying to remember which one it was. Rachel and Kirsty exchanged confused glances. But Giselle rose into the air and gazed down at the scattered bottles. Then a swish of her wand sent fairy dust sprinkling down on all of the bottles, making them glow. Most of the sparkles faded, but a bottle that was lying on its own underneath a holly bush kept glowing.

"My bottle!" cried Giselle.

"Get it!" the tallest goblin squealed.

The goblins and Rachel ran for the bottle, but Kirsty remembered a ballet move that she had seen in class.

She sprang through the air in a magnificent *jeté*. It looked like she was doing a split in the air!

She landed beside the bottle and picked it up, but the taller goblin was already flinging himself at her. Kirsty threw the bottle as high into the air as she could.

"Giselle!" she cried.

Giselle zipped through the air and flung her arms around the bottle. Instantly, she and the bottle disappeared to Fairyland.

Rachel and Kirsty whirled around to face the goblins.

"It's gone," said Rachel. "Time to give up."

"Give it back!" the shorter goblin yelled. "Where have all the bottles gone?"

The girls looked around. The only bottle left was the ordinary one belonging to the goblins. The taller goblin clutched his head with both hands.

"She took it!" he wailed. "What are we going to do?"

"We have to fake it," said the shorter goblin in a panicky voice. "Maybe if we glued some glitter on this bottle?"

They stomped off, talking about how to fool Jack Frost, and Rachel and Kirsty hugged each other.

"We did it!" said Rachel. "We found Giselle's magic bottle!"

"Do you think that means the ballerinas in our class will be feeling better?" Kirsty asked.

They hurried back into the school to find out. As soon as they were inside the school, their magical boots and jackets disappeared, and they were back in their ballet outfits. The dizzy ballerina was gone, so the girls hurried back to class. The music was playing and the dancers of the *corps* were busy rehearsing.

"Look," said Rachel. "All the ballerinas who felt sick are back! Oh, Kirsty, it worked!"

The ballet teacher waved at them.

"Come and join in, girls," she called. "Lots to get through! The dancers are practicing the dance of the swans."

Her voice didn't sound croaky anymore. The girls knew that Giselle's magic bottle must be protecting all ballerinas again.

"I hope Jack Frost will leave Giselle

alone now," said Kirsty, as they went to join the ballerinas.

Rachel squeezed her hand. They both knew that Jack Frost didn't usually give up that easily.

"We'll be there to help Giselle if she needs us," she said. "And in the meantime, we've got a class to finish!"

The Ballet Bag

Contents

After the class, Rachel and Kirsty felt very hungry indeed. The *corps de ballet* rehearsal and the exciting adventure with Giselle had really worked up their appetites.

"Ooh, my stomach's rumbling," said Kirsty as she changed back into her regular clothes.

"It's almost lunchtime," said Rachel, looking at her watch.

Just then, the ballerinas who had performed the dance of the little swans came up to them.

"Hi, I'm Alex," said the dancer with red hair and freckles. "This is Samira, Olivia, and Ayesha. We were wondering if you'd like to have lunch with us in the cafeteria?"

"Thank you, we'd love to," said Kirsty with a smile.

The Castle Springs cafeteria was very different from the ones at Kirsty's and Rachel's schools. Some people were dressed in regular clothes. Some were in tights and leotards. Others jostled past them in tutus and beautiful costumes, wearing tiaras and feathers in their hair.

It was so interesting that the girls kept staring and forgetting to eat.

"You're so lucky to be at such an exciting school," said Kirsty to Ayesha.

Ayesha nodded and smiled.

"It *is* exciting," she said. "I feel very lucky to be here and do something I love so much every day. But it is very hard work, and we don't have as much free time as you do at an ordinary school.

We have to be careful to always eat healthy food, and we have to get up very early and go to bed early, too."

"Do you ever get homesick?" asked Rachel.

"I did at first," said Alex. "It's strange to be living away from home. But I've made some really good friends here, and now that we are in the *corps de ballet*,

there is no time to think about anything except *Swan Lake*!"

"We're really looking forward to the performance tonight," said Kirsty. "Are you feeling nervous?"

The four ballerinas exchanged glances and laughed.

"We're all very nervous indeed," said Olivia. "But that's part of the life of a ballerina. I think that being nervous helps us to dance better, because we work so hard to get it right."

Everyone was looking at Olivia as she spoke, but Rachel noticed something.

A small figure in a fluffy white coat was helping himself to the salad on Samira's plate.

"Hey!" cried Rachel, half rising from her seat.

The figure scampered away, spitting out the salad and muttering, "Yuck! Healthy stuff!"

Rachel and Kirsty exchanged glances.

"That was a goblin," Kirsty whispered as Rachel sat down again. "He was wearing the same coat as the ones we saw earlier in the yard."

"I wonder why he's still here," said Rachel. "I hope it doesn't mean more trouble for Giselle."

"Maybe we should look for him after lunch," said Kirsty. "We could try to find out if he's up to no good."

But before they could leave the table, the ballet school's prima ballerina, Penny, came to find them.

"I'd like to invite you to watch the principals rehearsing," she said.

Rachel and Kirsty gasped. They knew that the principals danced the most important parts in the ballet.

As they walked along beside Penny, she told them what to expect.

"I am dancing the lead role," she said. "That means that I appear as two different characters called Odette and Odile. Rupert Randall is dancing the role of Prince Siegfried."

Rachel remembered reading the story of *Swan Lake*.

"Prince Siegfried is in love with Odette, isn't he?" she asked.

"That's right," said Penny. "Odette is a princess who has been transformed into a swan by a sorcerer's magic spell, so she is dressed all in white. Odile is the daughter of the sorcerer, and she is magically disguised as Odette to trick Prince Siegfried. She is dressed all in black."

Rachel and Kirsty could hardly wait for the rehearsals to begin!

A Principal Problem

A little later, Rachel and Kirsty were sitting on a bench at the side of the rehearsal room.

"The scene is a grand costume ball at the royal palace," said the ballet teacher. "Odile and Prince Siegfried dance together, and then the prince tells everyone that he wants to marry Odile."

The music began and Rupert Randall sprang into the center of the room. He jumped so high that he almost seemed to be flying. Then Penny joined him. Standing on one leg, she whipped the other leg around, spinning on the spot.

"These are called *fouettés*," the ballet teacher told the girls. "Penny must do thirty-two in a row. The people in the audience will be counting them, and they will burst into applause when she finishes. It is a very difficult step, and it shows a ballerina's strength and skill."

But then something awful happened. Penny wobbled, staggered sideways, and fell down with a loud bump. The music stopped and everyone stared at her in shock.

"Are you all right?" asked Rupert, helping her to stand up.

Penny nodded, but she looked very upset.

"That has never happened before," she said. "I don't know what's wrong with me—I just couldn't remember what I was doing."

"Let's move on to another section," said the ballet teacher. "I'd like to see the *pas de deux* from Act Two, please."

Kirsty and Rachel knew that this was a scene where Prince Siegfried danced with Odette and fell in love with her. The music was slow and beautiful, and the dancing seemed perfect to the girls.

But the ballet teacher was frowning as she watched. Then, as Rupert lifted Penny above his head, his hands seemed to slip on her waist. She fell, but luckily she managed to land on her feet.

"I'm so sorry," said Rupert, looking pale. "I just seemed to lose all strength in my arms."

"You were both slightly out of time with the music," said the ballet teacher, looking worried. "There is a tradition that a bad rehearsal means a good opening performance. I hope it's true!"

"Something is wrong," said Rachel in a low voice.

"Kirsty, let's slip out and look for that goblin. We have to find out if Jack Frost has something to do with this!"

When the girls returned to the cafeteria, it was empty. The kitchen area had been locked up behind shutters. The only sound they could hear was the faint music from different classes around the school.

"Perhaps he's gone back out to the yard," said Kirsty.

They turned to leave, and then they heard a chair leg scraping on the wooden floor. "Someone's in here!"

Rachel exclaimed. "Quick, Kirsty, guard the door!"

Kirsty ran to the door and stood with her back to it. Now there was no way out. Rachel started to search the cafeteria, looking under tables and chairs.

"I know you're in here," she said. "Please stop hiding. We just want to talk to you."

Suddenly a table was shoved aside and the goblin sprinted away from Rachel toward the door. He skidded to a halt when he saw Kirsty.

"Get out of my way, you interfering human," he squawked. "You'll never find the ballet bag!"

"What do you mean?" asked Kirsty, as Rachel ran up to join her. "Whose ballet bag?"

"Mind your own business," said the goblin, sticking out his tongue. "Jack Frost is too smart for you and that silly ballet fairy."

He clamped his hand over his mouth, realizing that he had said too much. Rachel folded her arms.

"So Jack Frost has stolen Giselle's ballet bag?" she asked. "Where is it?"

The goblin shook his head, with his hand still over his mouth. Kirsty turned to Rachel and gave her a secret wink. "There's no point asking him, Rachel," she said. "He doesn't know anything about the ballet bag."

"Oh, yes I do," the goblin said in an offended voice. "I know everything."

The girls felt excited. Their plan was working—the goblin was getting annoyed!

A Trip to Fairyland

"Jack Frost wouldn't have told a little goblin like you where he is keeping the bag," said Rachel.

"He didn't have to tell me," said the goblin in a boastful voice. "I was there with him when he threw it down the well."

“But I bet you don’t know how to find the well,” said Kirsty. “Jack Frost wouldn’t trust you with that sort of important information.”

“It’s the well in the middle of Forget-me-not Glade, *actually*,” said the goblin. “So there!”

Rachel and Kirsty smiled at each other.

“Well, you certainly showed us,” said Rachel. “Sorry for not believing you.”

They opened the door and the goblin walked out with his nose in the air. As soon as he was out of sight, the girls hugged each other and jumped up and down in excitement. They had the information they needed!

“Now we have to find Giselle and tell her about the bag,” said Kirsty.

They opened the lockets they always wore around their necks. Each one contained a little fairy dust—just enough to transport them to Fairyland. They each took a pinch and sprinkled it over themselves. It glittered a dazzling silver color and then—*whoosh*—they had shrunk to fairy-size. Gossamer wings unfurled on their backs, and a swirling cloud of fairy dust lifted them off their feet. The sparkles surrounded them like a whirlwind.

"We're on our way to Fairyland!" cried Rachel.

A few seconds later, the girls were blinking in the bright sunshine. They were fluttering above the yard of the Fairyland Palace. Below, a stage had been set up in the middle of the yard. There was a semicircle of six golden chairs in front of the stage, padded with red plush velvet. Six fairies were sitting on the chairs. The girls recognized many of them—Sophia the Snow Swan Fairy, Holly the Christmas Fairy, Eva the Enchanted Ball Fairy, and Miranda the Beauty Fairy. The king and queen were on their thrones behind the golden chairs.

"Look, there's Giselle!" said Rachel.

The Christmas Ballet Fairy was standing on the stage beside Bethany the Ballet Fairy. They were talking with their heads close together.

"Everyone looks worried," said Kirsty. "Let's go down and tell them our

news," Rachel suggested. "Come on!"

They flew down and landed in front of the king and queen, dropping into low curtseys. Queen Titania smiled and rose to her feet.

"Quiet, please, everyone," she said in her gentle voice. "We have some very important visitors."

Giselle flew down from the stage and landed beside the girls, hugging them tightly.

"I'm so happy to see you," she said.

"Thank you for helping me to find my magic bottle this morning."

"You're welcome," said Rachel, hugging her in return. "Are you putting on a performance?"

"It's a special preview of the Christmas ballet for the king and queen and a few of our dance-loving friends," Giselle explained. "It's the main performance tonight. But something has gone wrong, and I can't understand it. My solo was a mess."

"Giselle tripped up and forgot her steps," said Queen Titania. "I have a feeling that something is very wrong, and I suspect that Jack Frost is behind it. You may have arrived just in the nick of time, Rachel and Kirsty. Maybe you can help Giselle investigate."

"We can do better than that!" said Kirsty. "There was a goblin in the Castle

Springs ballet school, and he told us that Jack Frost has stolen Giselle's ballet bag."

All the other fairies had gathered around to listen, and they started to gasp and chatter. Giselle looked shocked.

"My ballet bag makes sure that all rehearsals go well," she said. "Without it, this evening's performances will be ruined!"

Forget-me-not Glade

"Girls, it is very important that we find the bag," said Queen Titania. "Could you help Giselle look for it?"

"We know where it is!" said Rachel, squeezing Giselle's hand. "We tricked the goblin into telling us. Jack Frost has thrown it into a well in the middle of Forget-me-not Glade."

Giselle frowned, and looked around at the other fairies. Bethany shrugged, and the six fairy guests shook their heads.

"Are you sure that was the name?" asked Sophia. "I've never heard of it."

"That's what the goblin said," Kirsty replied. "Oh no, do you think he made it up?"

"I think that the goblin was telling the truth," said the queen, turning to the frog footman Bertram. "Please go to the

ancient library and bring me the oldest map of Fairyland."

In a short time, Bertram came back with a large scroll of yellowing paper. It was covered in dust, and it looked very old. Two other frog footmen carried a table between them.

"Thank you," said the queen, taking the scroll.

She blew the dust away and unrolled the paper on the table. Rachel, Kirsty, and all the fairies gathered around in

excitement. The ink had faded with age, but it was clearly an ancient map of Fairyland.

Using one slender finger to search across the map, the queen began to explain.

"Many years ago, the Fairyland Palace

was surrounded by a large forest," she said. "There were hundreds of glades and pools and secret clearings—and fairies used them for dances and feasts and relaxation. Ah yes, it is as I thought."

The queen's finger stopped over a little glade in a valley, and everyone peered closer. The swirly writing beside the glade was faint, but Rachel and Kirsty could just make out the words.

Forget-me-not Glade

"That's it!" cried Giselle, performing a joyful arabesque. "That's where Jack Frost hid my ballet bag!"

"But how do we get there?" asked Kirsty. "The map is so old that Fairyland has changed a lot."

"The glade is in the same place," said the queen.

She waved her wand, and a piece of paper fluttered down into Kirsty's hands.

"I have used a navigation spell to show you the way," said the queen. "Just follow the arrows on the paper, and they will take you there."

There was no time to lose. Waving good-bye to their fairy friends, Rachel, Kirsty, and Giselle rose up into the blue sky. Kirsty looked down at the paper that the queen had given her, and saw a green line appear with arrows moving forward.

"We have to go straight ahead," she said.

They zoomed off, following the moving arrows on the map. Kirsty kept checking it and telling Rachel and Giselle when they needed to fly left or right. They passed over tall trees and glittering pools. They crossed hills like small mountains. But at last they reached a place where the land dipped down into a valley, and the arrows guided them down into a little wood of pine trees, tipped with snow. They landed on the edge of a snow-covered meadow at the heart of the woods. It was edged with baby pine trees, and there was a little stone well in the center.

"Oh no," Rachel said with a groan. The well was guarded by two goblins! "What are we going to do?" she whispered.

Rachel shrugged, but Giselle looked determined. "Let's get closer," the fairy said.

A Squabble and a Dance

The goblins were squabbling fiercely, and the fairies strained to hear what they were saying.

"But it's *my* turn to see Frostyev and the Goblinovski Festival Ballet," the skinny goblin wailed. "It's a one time performance!"

"You don't know anything about ballet," said the second goblin. "I'm an expert, so I should be the one to go."

"Why can't we just both go?" complained the skinny goblin.

"You know why!" squawked the second goblin. "Jack Frost ordered us to always leave one guard here, and that should be *you*."

"You!" screeched the skinny goblin.

"You!"

"*You*!"

The goblins were standing on opposite sides of the well, glaring at each other. The fairies could not fly into the well without being seen. Giselle looked up at the sky, and saw that the sun was beginning to set.

"We have planned our Christmas ballet for this evening," she said. "Without my ballet bag it will be hopeless, and time is running out."

"I've got an idea," said Kirsty. "We need to distract the goblins, and it sounds like they both love ballet. Giselle, could you do a dance for them?"

A little smile replaced Giselle's worried frown.

"I don't think they would want to see a fairy dance," she said. "But I think that some of these trees might be able to help."

She waved her wand toward the baby trees that surrounded the glade. Fairy dust flew from the tip and swirled upward. Some of it sprinkled down on the trees, while the rest turned into musical notes that hung in the air. Enchanting music began to play—faintly at first, and then gradually getting louder. The goblins stopped squabbling.

"Can you hear that?" asked the second goblin.

"Sounds like ballet music," said the skinny one.

Then their mouths dropped open. All around the glade, the baby trees began to sway to the music. They glided forward through the snow, lifting up their delicate branches like arms and shaking white snowflakes all around them.

The goblins stared in wonder as the trees twirled and swayed around them. The music grew louder and the goblins stepped away from the well, clasping their hands together as they gazed at the trees. They didn't see that Giselle was hovering on the edge of the glade, directing the trees with her wand like an orchestra conductor.

"Now's our chance!" she whispered to Rachel and Kirsty.

Rachel instantly zoomed toward the well and flew down into the darkness. Kirsty waited, holding her breath.

The seconds ticked by. Then, just when she thought that something must have gone wrong, Rachel shot out of the well with the ballet bag in her arms.

The enchanted music ended at once, and the trees slid back to their places. Puzzled, the goblins looked around and saw the three fairies.

"Go away!" screeched the skinny goblin.

"You can't have the bag," said the second goblin, blowing a raspberry at them.

"We already have it," said Rachel, handing the bag to Giselle.

Horrified, the goblins let out wails of rage.

"You tricky fairies!" shrieked the second goblin. "You'll be sorry! Jack Frost will get his revenge on you!"

They trudged off through the snow, and Rachel and Kirsty turned to Giselle.

"What do you think they meant by that?" asked Kirsty.

"Don't worry," said Giselle in an airy voice. "There is nothing that Jack Frost can do to me now. As long as my ballet shoes are safe, everything will be all right. And my ballet shoes are under guard in the palace, so nothing can possibly go wrong."

Giselle tapped the girls' lockets with her wand and filled them with fairy dust again. Then she smiled at both girls.

"You have saved tonight's performances," she said. "Thank you from the bottom of my heart. Now it is time for me to send you home so that you can enjoy *Swan Lake*."

Rachel and Kirsty were very happy to have been able to help Giselle again. But they couldn't help wondering what Jack

Frost would say when he heard about the ballet bag! The goblins were going to be in big trouble when they got back to the Ice Castle. Hopefully, Jack Frost had learned his lesson and would leave Giselle's ballet slippers alone!

The Silver Ballet Shoes

Contents

Backstage at the Ballet

"I can't remember the last time I've had such a busy day," said Rachel. "We've watched the rehearsals for *Swan Lake*, and we've helped Giselle get her magic water bottle and ballet bag back from Jack Frost."

"The day isn't over yet," said Kirsty. "We still have tonight's performance of *Swan Lake* to watch. I can't wait!"

The best friends were standing backstage, watching the dancers and crew prepare for the ballet. During their day at the Castle Springs Ballet School, they had made friends with the prima ballerina, Penny. She had said that they could stay backstage until just before the ballet began.

It was very exciting to be backstage. Kirsty and Rachel stood out of the way and watched as dancers dashed past in a flurry of tutus and feathery costumes. The props manager was preparing everything the dancers would need, and the wardrobe designer was following

the ballerinas around with a needle and thread, making last-minute alterations and repairs. The lighting was dim, but everywhere they looked the girls could see the sparkle of glitter on tutus and diamonds on tiaras.

"The stage is just over there," said Kirsty, pointing to the right. "Should we go and look at the scenery for the first act?"

"Ooh yes, let's!" said Rachel at once.

They tiptoed onto the stage. Thick velvet curtains hung between them and the audience, but they could hear the shuffle of hundreds of feet and the rustle of theater programs. Above the hum of chatter from the crowd, the girls could also hear the squeaks, toots, and pings of the orchestra tuning up their instruments.

The scenery showed the yard of a royal palace. Roses, lilies, and trees surrounded a sunny courtyard, while the palace in the distance was gleaming white.

"The theater's painters must be so artistic," said Kirsty. "I thought it wouldn't look as pretty up close as it does when you're in the audience, but it's perfect."

She traced over a picture of climbing pink roses with her finger. She could see every thorn and petal.

"I suppose it has to look beautiful for the dancers, too," said Rachel. "Oh, that's pretty!"

She picked up a golden bow, which was lying on a white table.

"That's the present that the queen gives to the prince in the first act," said Kirsty, remembering the start of the story.

Rachel rose onto her toes and raised her leg behind her, as she had seen the prince do in rehearsals. Then she lifted the bow above her head. There was a musical twang and a golden arrow flew into the air.

"Oh!" Rachel exclaimed. "How did that happen? I didn't do it!"

The arrow fell back down toward them, shining like a golden wand.

"That's not an arrow," cried Kirsty. "It's Giselle!"

The Christmas Ballet Fairy was pirouetting down, her wand raised above her head.

"Oh girls," said Giselle, holding out her arms to them. "I'm sorry to

interrupt your evening, but I have some terrible news!"

Rachel and Kirsty shared a worried glance. Jack Frost must be up to no good again!

Goblins and Guards

"What happened?" asked Rachel.

"I bet it has something to do with Jack Frost," said Kirsty.

"You're right," Giselle replied. "I should have paid more attention to the goblins' warning, but I was so sure that my ballet shoes were safe in the palace. While we were warming up for the

Christmas ballet performance, Jack Frost and his goblins arrived at the palace. I'll show you exactly what happened."

She waved her wand, and a shimmery moving picture appeared on the red stage curtain. It looked like someone was projecting a movie onto the velvet. The girls could see four mice standing guard outside a large wooden door. The guards looked very serious and handsome. Each one was wearing a tunic of red and gold, with a brown belt around the middle. From each belt hung a golden horn. On their heads the mice were wearing three-cornered red-and-gold hats.

As Rachel and Kirsty watched, a group of goblins scampered up to the

guards. They were all wearing tutus, and they were shouting. They leapt up and down in front of the guards, waving their arms and trying to pull off the three-cornered hats.

"Catch them!" ordered one of the guards.

At this, the goblins scattered in all directions and the guards chased after them. While the door was unguarded, Jack Frost tiptoed up to it. None of the guards saw him—they were too busy trying to control the goblins. Jack Frost pointed his wand at the lock, and the door swung open. He crept inside, and came out a few seconds later with a pair of ballet shoes in his hand.

"Frostyev and the Goblinovski Festival Ballet will dance again tonight!" he cackled.

The picture faded as Giselle turned to look at the girls.

"Those are my magic ballet shoes," she said, her wings drooping slightly. "As soon as we heard what had happened, the king and queen sent the Dance Fairies to the Ice Castle, but there was no one there. We have no idea where to look, and Christmas ballets everywhere are about to start. As long as Jack Frost has my magic shoes, all ballets will be ruined. What are we going to do?"

Before the girls could reply, they heard shouting from the side of the stage.

“Something’s wrong,” said Rachel. “Come on!”

Giselle tucked herself under a lock of Rachel’s hair and the girls hurried to see what all the shouting was about. They found the director surrounded by dancers and backstage crew, all looking angry and upset.

“Who took my costume?” the dancer playing the queen was wailing.

“My shoes are stained!” one of the younger ballerinas cried out.

“My props box is a mess!” a stagehand was shouting.

“Half the swans’ tutus are missing,” complained the costume designer.

The director held up her hands and then put them over her ears.

“Please, stop shouting!” she said. “This is a disaster! Why is everything going wrong? Everyone must start searching

the dressing rooms, from the stagehands to the prima ballerina herself. Hurry! If these problems aren't sorted out in the next half hour, I am going to have to cancel the performance."

Rachel and Kirsty exchanged looks of alarm.

"We can't let that happen," Kirsty said in a determined voice. "So many people have been looking forward to this ballet."

"Including us," added Rachel. "Christmas Eve will be ruined unless we

can get the ballet shoes in the next half hour!" The two friends had no time to lose. They had to find Giselle's magic ballet shoes—and fast!

Frostyev Onstage

Rachel and Kirsty hurried down dimly lit hallways until they reached the dressing rooms. All of the doors were open, and people were rushing in and out of the rooms in a panic.

"Just keep looking, everyone!" the costume designer said, hurrying along behind the girls. "We have to find those missing costumes."

"Can we help?" Kirsty asked her.

But the costume designer didn't hear her. She swept past the girls and started rummaging through a rack of tutus in the hallway. Rachel took a step forward to try to get her attention.

"Wait," said Kirsty, grabbing Rachel's arm. "Look!"

Someone in a tutu was just disappearing around the end of the hallway.

"That's odd," said Rachel. "Who could be leaving when the director has ordered everyone to stay here and search the dressing rooms for the missing tutus?"

"Let's find out," said Kirsty.

The girls hurried along the hallway, but when they turned the corner they only caught a glimpse of the mystery dancer's tutu as it disappeared around another corner. On and on the dancer led them, turning left and right through the maze of backstage hallways.

"I think we're heading back toward the stage," said Rachel eventually.

They rounded another corner and arrived back beside the stage. The curtain was still down, but the stage was now filled with a flurry of dancers in sparkling white tutus. They were rehearsing, but they were not ordinary ballerinas. The legs that stretched out behind them were green, and their heads were bald underneath their glimmering tiaras. They were goblins!

"It's the Goblinovski Festival Ballet—Jack Frost's ballet company!" said Kirsty. "They're here!"

"And they're wearing the missing tutus," Rachel added.

Giselle peered out from underneath Rachel's hair.

"That's not all," she said in a low voice. "Jack Frost is here, too—as Frostyev!"

Through a gap in the crowd of goblin dancers, they could see Frostyev standing on one leg, with the other leg pointing straight up in the air. He was wearing a tight silver costume and there were silver spangles in his hair and beard.

"I'm the best dancer in the world!" he declared, cackling with laughter. "And the smartest, too!"

“Dance some more! Dance some more!” squealed the goblins, clapping their hands together and jumping up and down.

Frostyev pirouetted across the stage with his arms above his head. Even though Rachel and Kirsty were worried, they couldn’t help noticing that he was dancing very well.

"While those silly fairies are searching for me at the Ice Castle, I'll be giving a bunch of silly humans the performance of a lifetime," Frostyev told the goblins. "They'll all be talking about me. No one will ever want to see another dancer, because I am so perfect and such an icy genius!"

"What if the humans don't realize how great you are?" asked one of the goblins.

Frostyev stopped pirouetting and scowled.

"If they don't clap then I will have fun turning them all into toads!" he snapped.

He sprang into the air so high that he seemed to be flying. His feet were beside the goblins' heads, and Giselle gave a horrified gasp.

"He's wearing my ballet shoes!" she cried. "That's why his dancing is so perfect. Nothing can stop him now!" Giselle's wings drooped and she looked very sad.

An Unexpected Interview

The goblins were getting bored of listening to Frostyev's boasting. Three of them hurried over to the red velvet curtain.

"Let's peek at the audience and make faces at them," suggested a short goblin with dirt on his face.

They huddled together and peered underneath the curtain.

"Oh dear, I hope no one sees them," said Kirsty. "I heard that there are going to be some journalists and ballet critics here tonight. It would be terrible if a photo of the goblins got into the newspapers."

"Oh!" Rachel exclaimed. "That gave me an idea. Giselle, could you disguise us as journalists? If we can flatter Frostyev and distract him, we might be able to get your shoes back."

"Oh, yes, please try!" said Giselle, clasping her hands together.

A few minutes later, Rachel and Kirsty walked onto the stage looking very different indeed. Rachel was wearing sunglasses and had a camera slung around her neck. Her hair was hidden under a pink beret. Kirsty's hair was piled up on top of her head and decorated with sparkling butterfly clips. She was wearing a purple jumpsuit with strings of beads around her neck, and carrying a notebook and pen.

Frostyev stopped dancing and glared at them.

"Who are you?" he demanded in a rude voice.

"Ooh, it's really him!" exclaimed Rachel, putting her hand over her heart. "The one and only Frostyev! I'm so excited I can hardly breathe!"

"We're from *Exclusively Ballet*, the best-selling ballet magazine," said Kirsty, holding out her hand. "We're dying to interview you for our next issue. You're the most amazing dancer we have ever seen."

Frostyev gave a smug little smile and shook her hand.

"Your sales will double with a picture of *me* on the cover," he said.

"Our readers will want to know everything about you," Rachel added. "How do you leap so high? How do you stay so handsome?"

"Well..." said Frostyev.

"What are your beauty secrets?" Kirsty went on. "Where do you have your beard trimmed?"

"I have never—" Frostyev began.

"And of course the most interesting question of all," said Rachel, talking over him. "*Why* do you tie your ballet shoe ribbons in such an old-fashioned way?"

Frostyev drew himself up to his full height and narrowed his eyes.

"What do you mean, 'old-fashioned'?" he demanded in a huffy voice. "I'm the latest and the greatest, and don't you forget it. I'm the freshest, most up-to-date dancer in the whole world."

"But none of the modern ballet dancers tie their ribbons that way," said Kirsty, pointing to the ribbons criss-crossing his feet. "I'll show you the new way if you want."

"Yes, do it right now," Frostyev ordered. "I can't perform if I look unfashionable."

He sat down and stuck out his legs. Kirsty crouched down beside him and Rachel crossed her fingers behind her back. Would her best friend be able to untie the shoes before Frostyev realized who they really were? Working quickly,

Kirsty carefully untied the long ribbons. Frostyev was expecting her to re-tie them, so this was the most dangerous moment of the plan. She had to be really fast!

Everyone's Perfect Christmas

Kirsty tried to pull the shoes off gently, so that Frostyev wouldn't notice. But they were clamped tightly around his bony feet, and he frowned at her.

"What are you doing?" he asked, bringing his face closer to hers.

Kirsty shivered as she looked into his cold, pale eyes.

“Wait a minute, I recognize you!” he exclaimed.

“Kirsty, quickly!” cried Rachel.

With a hard tug, Kirsty yanked the ballet shoes from Frostyev’s feet. He threw himself at her, but she had just enough time to hurl the shoes into the air as he knocked her backward.

Giselle zoomed out of the shadows and grabbed one of the shoes, while Rachel leapt up to catch the other. She handed it to Giselle, and the shoes instantly shrank to fairy size. At the same moment, the tutus and tiaras vanished from the goblin dancers. Rachel and Kirsty smiled at each other. Everything was returning to normal.

A flurry of sparkling fairy dust surrounded Frostyev, and a few seconds later his ballet costume disappeared. He

was Jack Frost again. He scrambled to his feet and shook his fist at them.

"Give me back those shoes!" he yelled at Giselle, who was fluttering above his head.

"Absolutely not," she replied. "They are my shoes and you stole them. You have been very mean, trying to ruin the fun of Christmas ballets, but it hasn't worked—thanks to Rachel and Kirsty."

The little fairy smiled at the girls, whose journalist disguises had now disappeared.

"But what am I supposed to do?" Jack Frost demanded. "The Goblinovski Festival Ballet can't perform now."

"Go back to your Ice Castle where you are needed," said Giselle in a gentle voice. "It's wintertime, and your snow and ice are very important."

Jack Frost stared at her for a moment, and then raised his wand in the air.

"Come on," he snapped at the goblins. "There's work to be done. Stop messing around here and come with me!"

The goblins gathered around him.

"Merry Christmas, Jack Frost," said Giselle.

For a moment, a little smile hovered around Jack Frost's mouth.

"Merry Christmas," he said in a gruff voice.

There was a bright blue flash, and then Jack Frost and his goblins vanished from the stage. All that remained were a few melted snowflakes, which Giselle dried with a wave of her wand.

"Thank you, Rachel and Kirsty," she said. "Now I can make sure that tonight's performances are a huge success.

I must return these shoes to Fairyland in time for the curtain call. Merry Christmas to you both!"

"Merry Christmas, Giselle!" called the girls.

As the little fairy disappeared, the director hurried onstage toward the girls.

"Good news!" she said. "All the costumes have been found! Hurry to your seats now, girls—the ballet is about to start."

Kirsty and Rachel ran to find their seats as the orchestra began to play the opening music. They saw their parents waving to them, and sat down just in time. The curtain rose to reveal a bustling birthday scene, with the handsome prince at the center of the celebrations.

"This is going to be the ballet of the year!" Mrs. Walker murmured to the girls.

"And a really magical end to our ballet adventures," Kirsty whispered. "Merry Christmas, Rachel."

"Merry Christmas, Kirsty," Rachel replied. "I'll never forget a single moment!"

THE STORYBOOK FAIRIES

Rachel and Kirsty found Giselle's missing magic objects. Now it's time for them to help…

Elle
the Thumbelina Fairy!

Join their next adventure in this special sneak peek…

Into the Pages

The other fairies jumped up and smiled at Rachel and Kirsty.

"It's wonderful to meet you," Rachel said, recovering from the surprise of being whisked to Fairyland. "But why have you brought us here?"

"I'm afraid that Jack Frost and his goblins have done something truly terrible," said Elle, sinking into one of the chairs.

She raised her wand and pointed it at one of the bookshelves. A large book swept itself off the shelf, opened in midair, and showed a big, blank page. As it hovered there, blurry pictures began to appear on the page. The pictures grew clearer and the girls drew in their breaths.

"It's a picture of this library," said Kirsty.

"With Jack Frost and his goblins sneaking around inside," Rachel added. "What did they do?"

"They took our most precious belongings," said Elle.

The girls watched the picture in the book. Jack Frost undid the golden clasp of a wooden box. He raised the lid and scooped the contents into a bag, laughing. Then he handed the bag to a goblin, threw the box on the floor, and left the library.

The picture faded and the book closed itself and slotted back into its place on the shelf.

"What was in the box?" asked Rachel.

"Four magical objects that have power over the stories we protect," said Elle. "They give the holder control of the stories. We use them to make sure that the stories go as they are supposed to, so every story ends well."

"What is Jack Frost using them for?" Kirsty asked.

“He and his goblins are using our magical objects to actually go *into* the stories and change them,” said Elle. “They want the stories to be all about them.”

Kirsty and Rachel exchanged a worried glance.

RAINBOW magic™ SPECIAL EDITION

Which Magical Fairies Have You Met?

- ❑ Joy the Summer Vacation Fairy
- ❑ Holly the Christmas Fairy
- ❑ Kylie the Carnival Fairy
- ❑ Stella the Star Fairy
- ❑ Shannon the Ocean Fairy
- ❑ Trixie the Halloween Fairy
- ❑ Gabriella the Snow Kingdom Fairy
- ❑ Juliet the Valentine Fairy
- ❑ Mia the Bridesmaid Fairy
- ❑ Flora the Dress-Up Fairy
- ❑ Paige the Christmas Play Fairy
- ❑ Emma the Easter Fairy
- ❑ Cara the Camp Fairy
- ❑ Destiny the Rock Star Fairy
- ❑ Belle the Birthday Fairy
- ❑ Olympia the Games Fairy
- ❑ Selena the Sleepover Fairy
- ❑ Cheryl the Christmas Tree Fairy
- ❑ Florence the Friendship Fairy
- ❑ Lindsay the Luck Fairy
- ❑ Brianna the Tooth Fairy
- ❑ Autumn the Falling Leaves Fairy
- ❑ Keira the Movie Star Fairy
- ❑ Addison the April Fool's Day Fairy
- ❑ Bailey the Babysitter Fairy
- ❑ Natalie the Christmas Stocking Fairy
- ❑ Lila and Myla the Twins Fairies
- ❑ Chelsea the Congratulations Fairy
- ❑ Carly the School Fairy
- ❑ Angelica the Angel Fairy
- ❑ Blossom the Flower Girl Fairy

Find all of your favorite fairy friends at
scholastic.com/rainbowmagic

RMSPECIAL17